The Magical Tale of Santa Dust®

A Christmas Tradition

Written by: Patricia Cardello

Illustrated by: Manuela Soriani

"2018"

Dear Emily,

"Hope you start a new tradition"

Love & Kisses
Aby

This book belongs to: *Emily Hope Segui*

I began my Santa Dust tradition on: _____

N & J Publishing
New York

Once upon a Christmas Eve, on a quiet street where street lamps seldom flickered, two small children, a boy and his sister, sat looking out their window at the darkening sky that Santa would be flying across later that night.

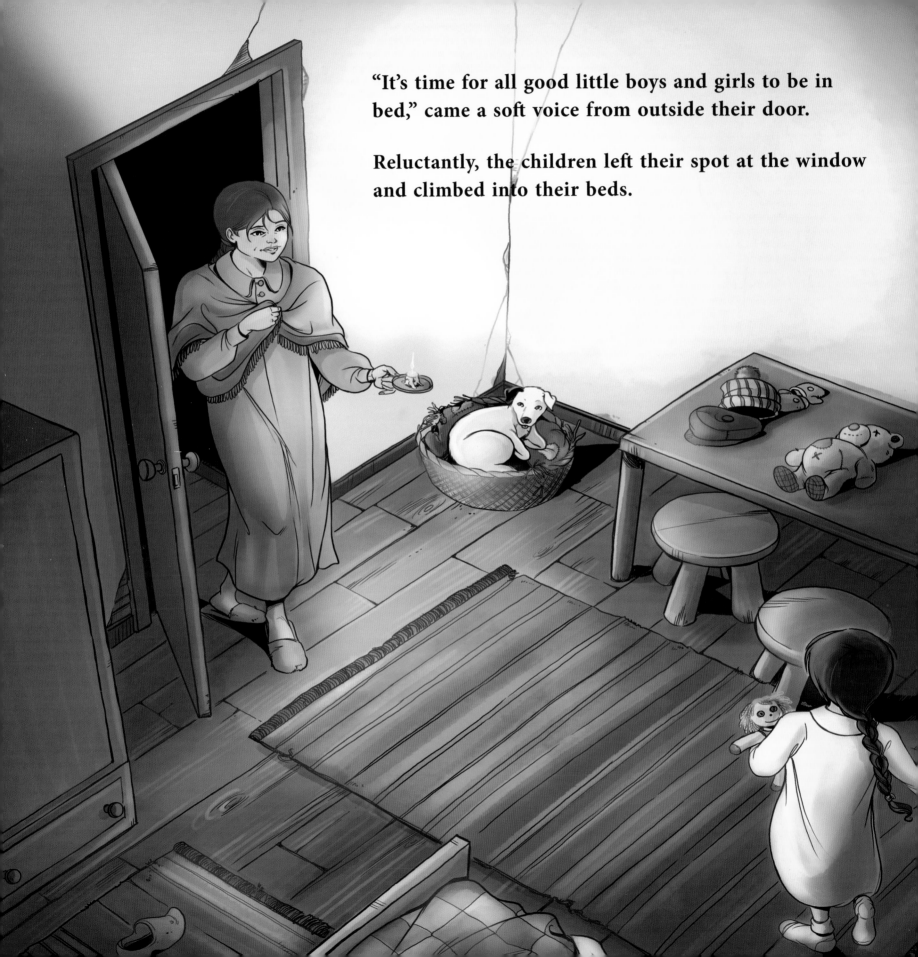

"It's time for all good little boys and girls to be in bed," came a soft voice from outside their door.

Reluctantly, the children left their spot at the window and climbed into their beds.

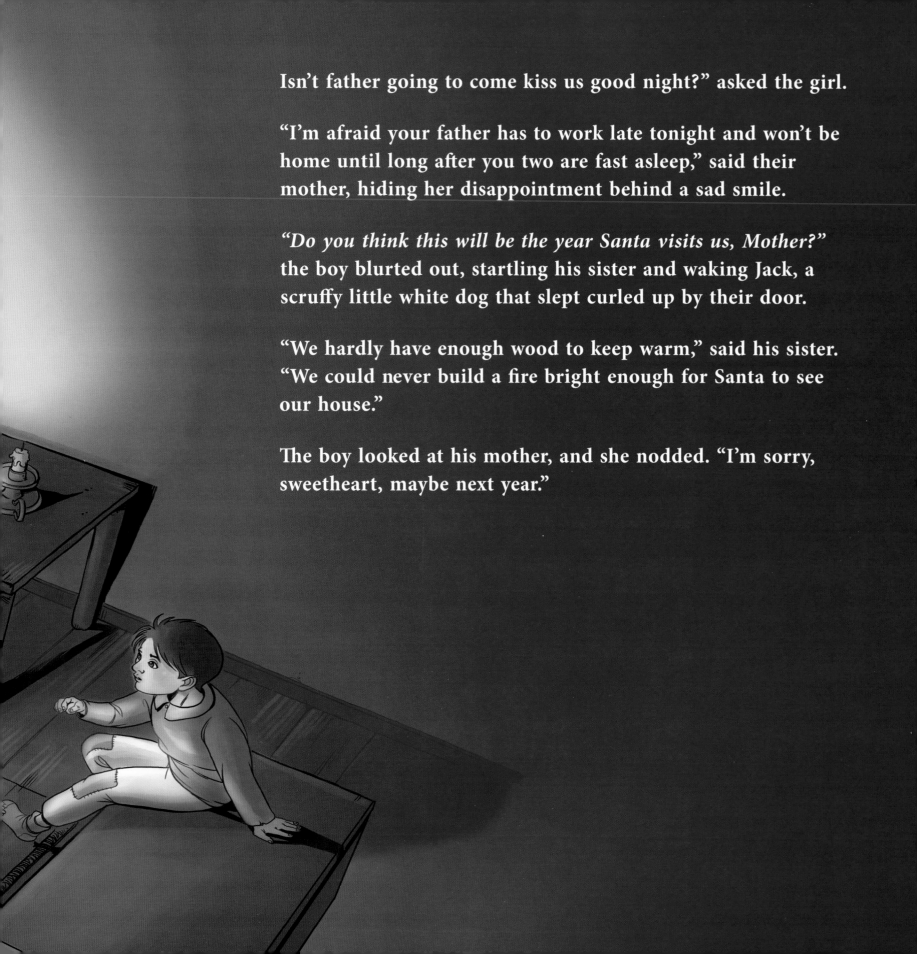

Isn't father going to come kiss us good night?" asked the girl.

"I'm afraid your father has to work late tonight and won't be home until long after you two are fast asleep," said their mother, hiding her disappointment behind a sad smile.

"Do you think this will be the year Santa visits us, Mother?" the boy blurted out, startling his sister and waking Jack, a scruffy little white dog that slept curled up by their door.

"We hardly have enough wood to keep warm," said his sister. "We could never build a fire bright enough for Santa to see our house."

The boy looked at his mother, and she nodded. "I'm sorry, sweetheart, maybe next year."

Tears stung the boy's eyes, and he fought to keep them from spilling onto his cheeks.

"But we've been so good," he said softly.

"You are always good," his mother replied. "If Santa knew you were here, I'm sure he would bring you all the presents you deserve."

The boy turned to face the wall, so his mother and sister wouldn't see him cry.

His mother bent down to kiss him on the cheek.

"Good night, Children," whispered their mother as she tucked them into their beds and quietly shut the door behind her.

That night, as the boy slept, dreaming of elves and presents, a strange noise awakened him.

He opened his eyes to find Jack pawing at the window and whimpering at something outside.

The boy looked out the window into the faint moonlight, but only saw the silhouettes of trees and the hard-packed snow on the ground.

"Hush, Jack," the boy scolded, but the dog wouldn't be quiet.

So the boy pulled his thin coat over his pajamas to carry Jack outside.

No sooner had the boy opened the door when Jack leapt from his arms and ran full speed into the bushes.

"Jack! Jack!" the boy called out in a loud whisper, hoping not to wake his sister. Finally, after what felt like an eternity, Jack came bursting out of the bushes and jumped into the little boy's arms.

Jack was wet from the snow, and the boy began to shiver.

But as he held his breath in the quiet of the night, he heard a happy little voice giggling in the bushes Jack had just come out of—followed by the sound of tiny little feet running across the snow.

The boy turned and fled into the house.

"Where have you been?" asked his sister as the boy burst into their room.

"Jack heard something outside. . ." began the boy, but he was quickly interrupted by his sister.

"What's in Jack's mouth?" the girl cried excitedly.

In the dog's mouth was a fancy red pouch. It looked expensive and out of place in their modest bedroom.

"Let's open it," said the boy.

"I'm not going to touch it," his sister protested. "It has Jack's drool on it!"

The boy abruptly snatched it from the dog's mouth and shook it near his ear. A musical jingling came from the pouch, and their eyes grew wide.

Slowly, as the boy opened the pouch, a bright light flashed before their eyes.

From inside the pouch he pulled out a silver glass ball covered in snowflake designs that seemed to move as they sparkled, lighting up the room.

"What is it?" whispered his sister.

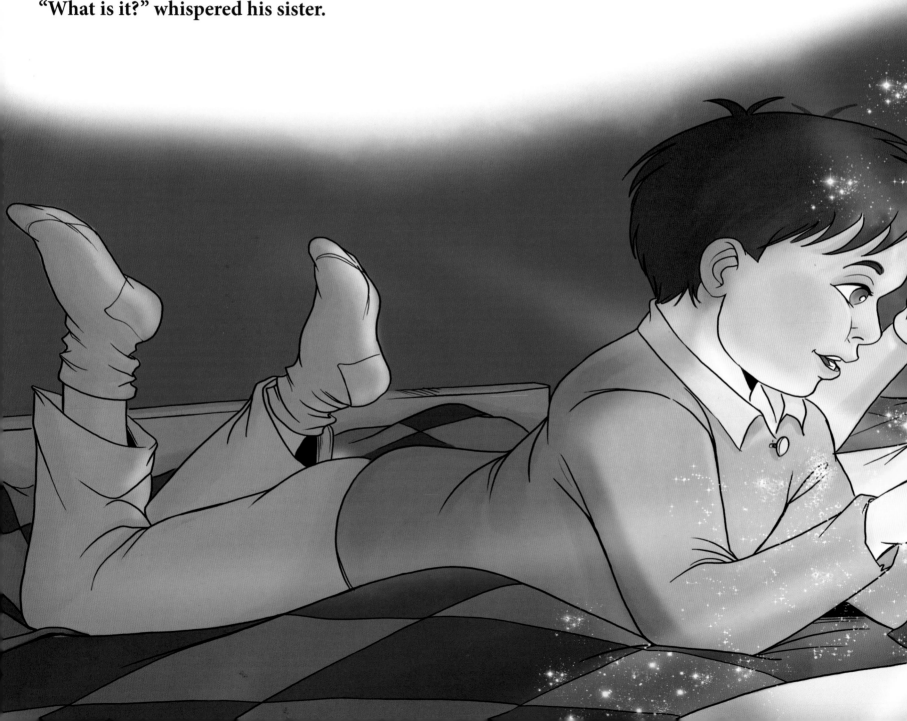

"I don't know," said the boy. "It looks like a Christmas tree ornament full of some kind of dust."

"It's beautiful," said the girl. "But how does it sparkle so bright with so little light?"

"It must be magical!" said the boy.

Then the girl got an idea. "If we can hang it from the highest peak on the chimney outside, Santa will see the sparkle and is sure to find us!"

She grabbed her brother's coat and handed it to him.

"Santa is going to come this year, Brother. I just know it! I believe that Santa will find us," the girl said in awe as she and Jack climbed onto the boy's red sled.

The boy didn't reply, not
wanting to get his hopes up.

"This is the best spot to climb onto the roof," said the boy, rubbing his hands together. "Give me the ornament."

But when his sister was taking the ornament out of its pouch,
it slipped from her fingers and burst on the ground with a
surprising little *pop*.

The boy and girl stared down as a shimmering silver
dust—all that was left of the ornament—floated around the
ground, where it stayed, sparkling in the moonlight.

"Oh no!" cried the girl. "Now Santa will never find us!"

Later that night, as the two children and their dog lay sleeping in their beds, Santa's sleigh flew swiftly through the night sky on his yearly journey overhead.

"Whoa!" Santa cried out when he spotted a familiar sparkling in the darkness below.

Then he shook his reins, guiding his reindeer down for a closer look.

That was when Santa saw a house
he had never seen before!

He brought his sleigh to a stop on the snow-packed roof, and on silent footsteps, he shimmied down the chimney with his magical sack over his shoulder.

Inside the house, Santa found the red pouch where the boy had left it and chuckled to himself.

It was one of the many red pouches Santa's elves kept their own magical Christmas tree ornaments in. He wondered which elf would be missing an ornament when he got back to the North Pole - and chuckled again.

Without a sound, Santa opened his sack, reached in, and pulled out a fat little Christmas tree, complete with decorations, and placed it in a dusty corner of the room.

He then took out five presents—one for each member of the family, including a bone for Jack.

Then, almost as an afterthought, Santa took a small blue card out of his pocket. As he gently blew across its surface, a silvery dust sprinkled through the air.

As Santa reached out to catch the dust, a poem appeared on the card in tiny gold letters:

Sprinkle on the ground at night
The moon will make it sparkle bright
Santa's reindeer fly and roam
this will lead him to your home!

Santa collected the dust and poured it into the red pouch. He then attached the card to the pouch and hung it on the tree.

"*Santa Dust!*" he whispered, tapping the pouch with his finger.

Then, just as Santa was turning to leave, Jack ran into the room to investigate.

Smiling, Santa put his finger to his lips, and Jack seemed to understand that all was well.

After Santa left, Jack ran back into the children's bedroom and hopped onto the little boy's bed.

That night Jack slept soundly knowing that, in the morning, the children would be waking to their very first visit from Santa.

And, as Jack slept, he wondered how many other boys and girls around the world would be waking on Christmas morning to the magic of Santa Dust.

Believe

Copyright © 2011 Patricia Cardello
PACardello@aol.com

Third Edition
Library of Congress Control Number: 2011904212—ISBN: 978-0-9833662-2-5
Illustrations and Interior Design: Manuela Soriani—arcemproject@yahoo.it
"Santa Dust" and "The Magical Tale of Santa Dust" are registered trademarks of PAC Jennic Inc.

Printed in the China.

N & J Publishing
200 North End Avenue Suite #18D, New York, New York 10282, 212-260-7075, 212-330-7708
NandJPublishing@aol.com, themagicaltale@aol.com, www.themagicaltales.com